# The Silver Path

Published in 1993 by Magi Publications in association with
Star Books International, 55 Crowland Avenue, Hayes, Middx UB3 4JP
Co-produced with Lemniscaat b.v. The Netherlands
Text © 1993 by Christine Harris
Illustrations © 1993 by Helen Ong
The right of Christine Harris to be identified as the author
of this work has been asserted by her in accordance with
The Copyright, Designs and Patents Act 1988.
Printed and Bound in Belgium by Proost N.V. Turnhout
ISBN 1 85430 257 4

# The Silver Path

written by
## Christine Harris

Illustrated by
## Helen Ong

Magi Publications, London

TF

Dear Penny,

Thank you for your letter, and the photo you sent with it, to show me the lovely house where you live. You have such a big garden to play in with your dog Scruff.

In return, I am sending you with this letter a postcard of
the hotel where Mama and I are staying. This hotel is even
bigger than your house, I think! Do you see all the balconies,
one above the other, like a stack of open drawers?
Our balcony is right near the top. You will be able to find
it on the postcard, because I have marked it with a cross
inside a circle, like a target.

If I look over the wall of our balcony in the daytime
I can see the sea far below.
I close my eyes, and imagine I'm diving into the cool
blue water.

Back in our village, my friend Branko and I both won medals for diving.
I wish Branko had come with us to the hotel.
Mama says, "Well, I don't. I've got problems enough, with only one of you."

When night comes, the moon builds a silver path over
the sea, going all the way from where I am to where
you are, Penny.
I close my eyes and imagine I am running along the
silver path to meet you.

Mama sits in the room behind our balcony all day.
When I ask why doesn't she come out to look at the sea,
she says, "The sun is too bright for me out there."
But even when the sun goes in, she *still* stays indoors.
She tells me, "I have all this knitting to finish."

Mama is knitting another sweater for me, because I dropped my old one on the road somewhere, after we left the village. Mama says, "You should not have taken off your old sweater while you were walking, Niko."

"I was hot, then," I complain. And she says, "But you will be cold soon when winter comes."

The food we get in this hotel is very strange. Not at all like the lovely food you told me about in your letter, when you went for a picnic with your mum and dad.
Today, we had macaroni and tinned sardines.

I don't ever remember eating macaroni and tinned
sardines, back at home. I ask Mama, "Do you remember the
taste of the bread you used to bake in the oven at the far
end of the garden? Do you remember the honey from our beehive,
and how I used to spoon it over your fresh crusty bread?"

When I think of our garden, I can't help thinking of the
kennel Papa helped me to build there, for my little puppy.
I hated having to leave the puppy behind.

"Try to sleep, now," says Mama.
But it is hard to sleep, with babies crying in the next room
and an old woman coughing in the room below. Far away,
there are rumbling, grumbling bangs – like thunder.
"Do you remember how much louder the bangs were, back in
the village?" I ask Mama.
"No! No! No!" she shouts. I don't think she is answering me.
I think she is talking in her dreams.

Perhaps she is dreaming about the terrible day when soldiers marched into the cafe back in our village? They started to take away all the food, and Papa told them they should pay for what they took, like other people. That is why he is in a prison camp now, and why I have been sent with Mama to this hotel for refugees.

Mama says that one day, Papa will be free again. She says we
shall all return to the village together. Penny, I will be
so happy on that wonderful day! I am going to close my
eyes now, and imagine I have invited you to visit us. I'm going
to imagine the fun we'll both have.

Your friend,
Niko